99 Word Puzzles

Written by
Simon Tudhope and Sarah Khan

Designed by
Marc Maynard and Michael Hill

Illustrated by
Lizzie Barber and Non Figg

```
        H S F G N
      S P I N D T W E
    F L S A N D I U S H F
    C S F N G L W H R F C I
    R O E M I N R O T C O S
    H A R E E Y W H T L N R H
    R B F R T K A I B E R A
    S A N A E E E V R O I L L
  U L L E H S A R T E S O
    N G I E L E R O C H
    A S E A W E E D
      T S O J N
```

Word ladder

On each rung of the ladder, write a word that can be made by taking away one letter from the word above. Use the clues to help you.

STARTLING

Clue: Beginning something

Clue: Looking for a long time

Clue: You'll find this on a guitar.

Clue: Bees and wasps can do this.

Clue: Choirs and popstars do this.

Pirate challenge

Draw a circle around the words that **can't** be made from the letters in the word PIRATE using each letter only once.

PEST

ART

PLATE

TIE

PIT

RARE

EAT

AREA

RIPE

PAIR

TEAR

TEN

Word wheel

Write letters in the blank spaces of this wheel to finish the words. Use the clues at the bottom of the page to find the right answers. Read from the outside of the circle to the middle, so that each word ends with the letter 'N'. One word has been completed for you.

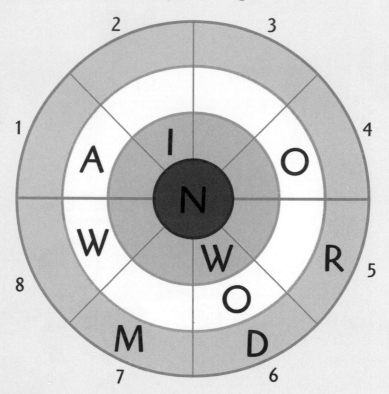

Clues

1. A farm building
2. A big smile
3. Opposite of fat
4. Another word for midday

5. Wet weather
6. Opposite of up
7. To complain
8. White water bird

Shape fill-in

Write the names of the shapes below into the grid.

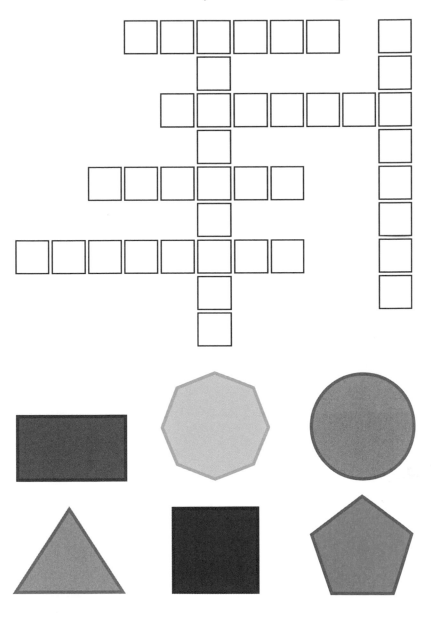

Blog entry

Patrick is about to post the message below on his blog.
Circle the spelling mistakes that should be picked up by
his spell check.

Paddy's blog

Today my dad was angry becouse I spendt my lunch money on a tenis ball. Nowon has a tenis ball. They always get losed so everyone will play with my ball. We had stu for diner. Yuck. Then I went to Neil's house and plade computer games. He always beets me but today I beet him. He said he losed on purpus! More scool tomoro.

Save   Delete   Send

Written in the stars

There are ten words associated with stars hidden in the letters below. Cross them out, then read across the rows to spell out a fourteen-letter word with the remaining letters.

```
                T
            C   L   S
            C   E   P
    O   S   B   N   L   S   A   S   L   S   T
    E   U   U   L   U   C   R   N   I   K   L
    N   R   S   S   O   K   I   G   Y
    N   H   T   P   L   G   H
    I   I   E   E   E   H   T
    N   N   R   A   T   T   G
    G   E   I       O   N   A
    S               S
```

Answer: ....

Word swirl

Draw lines to mark where one swirling word ends and another one begins. How many are there?

Answer: ....

Word web

The vowels on this web (A, E, I, O, U) are on sticky threads, and the other letters are on threads that are safe to walk on. Draw the route the fly should take to escape from the middle of the web without getting stuck. The letters you pass spell out three words. What are they?

Escape ⬅

Answers: ....

....

Broken words

These groups of letters are parts of words. Each word has been torn into three pieces, but one of the words has a piece missing. Which three letters would be on the missing piece?

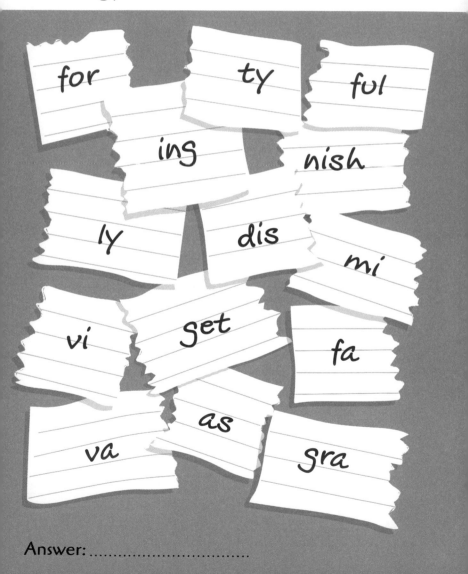

for ty ful

ing nish

ly dis

mi

vi get

fa

va as gra

Answer: ....

Duplicate

The grid is made up of nine blocks, each containing nine squares. Fill in the blank squares, so that each block, row and column contains all the letters of the word DUPLICATE.

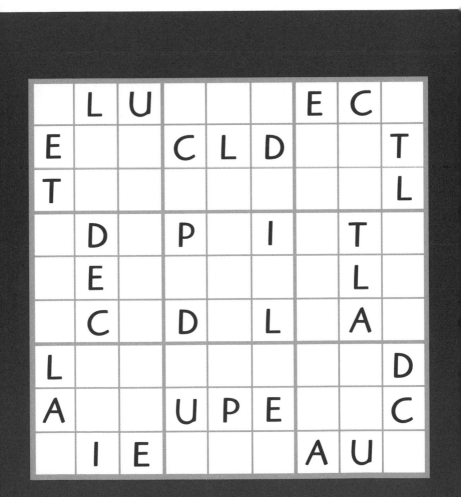

Camping crossword

Solve the clues and write the answers in the grid.
Each answer includes either the word CAMP or TENT.

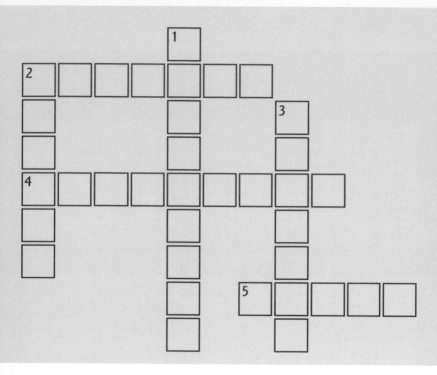

Across
2. Happy
4. What you are capable of achieving
5. A fraction

Down
1. Being held back after school
2. The grounds of a school or college
3. Run around playfully

Opposites attract

All but one of these words can be paired up with another one that has the **opposite** meaning. Circle the word that is on its own.

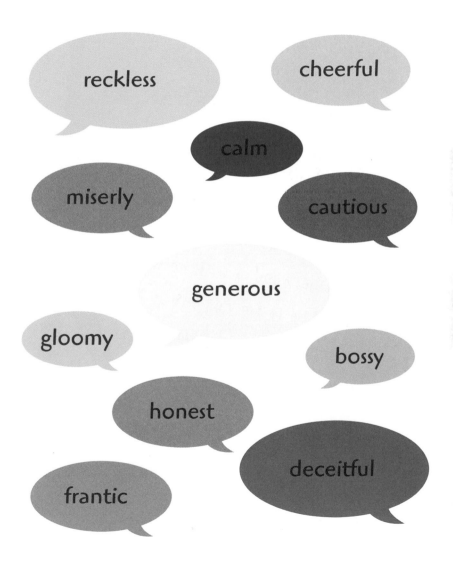

Spelling spotter

Circle the spelling mistakes in Ben's homework.

My heroe is Robbin Hood. He took monney from rich people who woudn't share even thow poor people were really hungry. He robed the rich to fede the por and campt out every nite with his frends in a big forest caled Sherwood. I wish he was alive 2day so we cud lite a fir and sing songs and I woud tell evryone that I was frends with Robbin Hood.

Ice hopping

The penguin can only hop onto the icebergs with nouns on them – the others are too slippery. Draw the shortest route across the safe icebergs to the land.

Word switch

In each line, circle the two words that need to switch places for all the words to be in alphabetical order.

1. gear   gate   gift   glad   gold

2. hand   help   hole   hint   hoop

3. make   mast   mist   mule   more

4. pack   pass   page   pink   pour

5. soap   sock   sold   soil   sown

6. tram   tray   trap   trim   true

Puzzle planet

Can you find the words below hidden in this planet-shaped grid?

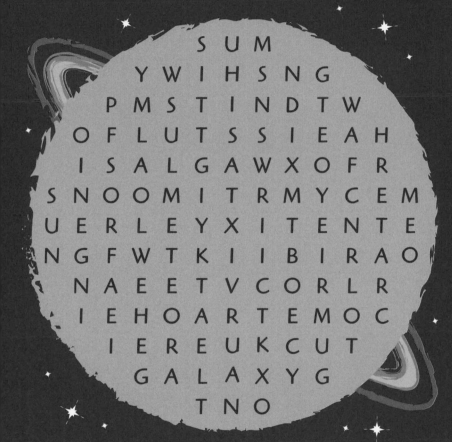

MOON   COMET   METEOR

SUN   GALAXY   GRAVITY

STAR   ORBIT   CRATER

Words in a word

Use the clues below to find some of the words that can be made from the letters in CONGRATULATIONS. No letter can be used more than the number of times it appears in the original word.

1. ....
Clue: A tune with lyrics (4 letters)

2. ....
Clue: A path, or to follow (5 letters)

3. ....
Clue: A sign (6 letters)

4. ....
Clue: Opposite of 'for' (7 letters)

5. ....
Clue: Animated drawings (8 letters)

Daisy chain

Can you change 'seed' to 'leaf'? Fill the blank flowers, following the chain. Change one letter at a time to form a new word in each flower.

seed

leaf

Double meanings

Complete each sentence by choosing one of the words from the bottom of the page. One word fits into both spaces in each sentence. Although the words in the two spaces will look the same, they'll have two different meanings. The first one has been done for you.

1. The violinist put on a......*live*...... concert in the town where she used to.......*live*..........

2. Her first album went down in the .... as one of the best-selling.....................in history.

3. After the concert, she put down her.....................
and took a ....

4. When she .... again, someone threw a red .... onto the stage.

minute	row	~~live~~	records
rose	lead	read	bow
tear	sow	project	contest

First and last

Each of these words starts and ends with the same letter.
Can you fill in the missing letters?

.... OMI ....AYHE...........

.... OYA ....EFEN...........

.... RAS .... IDO ....

.... RUS .... IOS ....

.... REN .... LUF ....

Cross e-word

Solve the clues, then put the words in the correct places in the grid. The 'E's have been filled in for you to help you decide which word goes where.

1. The way out
2. Finish
3. Give something to eat
4. Soft or sensitive
5. Opposite of wild
6. Your brother's or sister's daughter

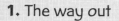
Wish you were here!

Word pairs

All but one of these words can be paired up with another one that has the **same** meaning. Circle the word that is on its own.

frail

looped

cloudy

active

curly

jump

overcast

weak

light

leap

lively

Butterfly maze

Help the butterfly find the shortest route to the flower.
Then, rearrange the letters you pass along the way to
spell out a word.

Answer: ....

Odd one out

Underline the word in each list that is the odd one out.

1. sleeping
   dozing
   loitering
   napping
   snoozing

2. tired
   sleepy
   exhausted
   alert
   weary

3. fantasize
   dream
   imagine
   create
   ignore

4. bright
   dark
   gloomy
   dim
   murky

5. quiet
   hush
   silence
   racket
   lull

6. rest
   lounge
   rush
   relax
   unwind

Which word?

1. Which of these words means 'a danger'?

HAZARD GIZZARD

WIZARD

BUZZARD

LIZARD BLIZZARD

2. Which of these words means 'to try'?

REVIVE

THRIVE

STRIVE

DEPRIVE

ARCHIVE

DERIVE

3. Which of these words is a shade of pink?

FUSILLI

FUSION

FUTON

FUCHSIA

FUTILE FUSSY

4. Which of these words means 'a piece'?

INACTION

FRACTION

FRICTION FACTION

REACTION

FICTION

Space scramble

Can you unscramble these groups of letters to find the names of six things you might find in space?

1. natlpe

4. oritsade

2. coertk

5. estlletia

3. sutanator

6. oteretmei

Corner letters

Find five words that can be made by combining **all** the corner letters with **any** of the letters in the middle. One of the words uses all eight letters.

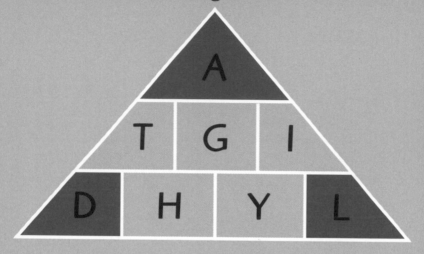

1. ....

2. ....

3. ....

4. ....

5. ....

Farm jumble

The words in each line can be rearranged to make a sentence. Write numbers under the words to show their correct order, writing '1' under the first, and so on.

1. grass. on sheep The munched

....

2. ducks in pond. the Two swam

....

3. the red on apples Big tree. hung

....

Front and back

When you split each of these four-letter words in half, they fit around one of the groups of letters below to make an eight-letter word. Can you find the words they make? The first one has been done for you.

SING   RENT   ~~MAIN~~   NOTE   HIND

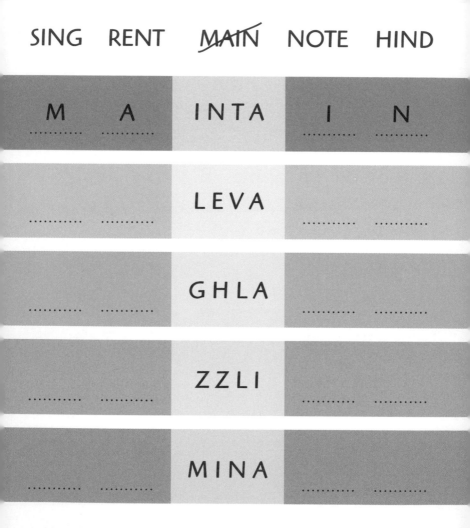

| M | A | INTA | I | N |

| | | LEVA | | |

| | | GHLA | | |

| | | ZZLI | | |

| | | MINA | | |

Book words

Complete the words in the circles that will join with the word 'book' to make a new word.

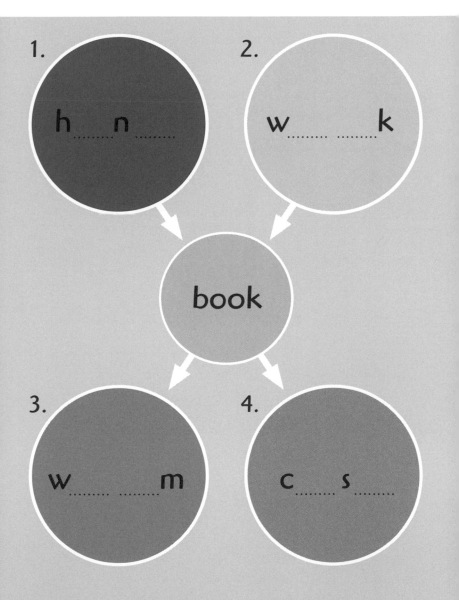

1. h......n.........

2. w......... ....k

book

3. w......... ....m

4. c......... s.........

Hidden insects

Underline the name of an insect hidden in each sentence.
The first one has been done for you.

1. I found the m**ap hid**den below deck.

2. I won't be coming; I'm otherwise engaged.

3. The tribe expected their new leader to be strong.

4. The boy was playing his guitar upstairs.

5. He ran to the other side.

6. She has a stall selling natural and organic cosmetics.

7. The bear wiggled as it danced.

8. He had to stifle a yawn as he pretended to listen.

Coded message

Complete the grid to make a sentence. Fill the squares
in each column with one of the letters from the column
above. Each letter is used once. Three grid squares have
been filled in for you.

Lily pads

Jumping from one lily pad to the next across the pond, this frog can spell out the kind of food he likes to eat most. Write the word at the bottom of the page.

Answer: ....

Cat rescue

Some letters are missing from this article in a local paper about a daring cat rescue. Fill them in below.

8 Thursday July 10th

"CATch!"

Scratchy the c … t has been rescued from the t … … … in front of Miss Jerry's h … … … … e, but our source tells us that things didn't go entirely to p … … … n. Fireman Flood went up with a cat box, but Scratchy refused to get inside and instead wrapped himself around Mr. Flood's f … … e. Another fireman went up to h … … p, but Scratchy scrambled down them both, leaped to the ground, and sauntered off with his h … … … d h … … … … h … … h.

Beach scramble

Can you unscramble these groups of letters to find the names of six things you might see at the beach?

1. csaedsltan

....

2. lahslees

....

3. rsfaisth

....

4. leshjlify

....

5. okocprlo

....

6. eaesdew

....

Kitchen anagrams

These words are anagrams – in each one, the letters can be rearranged to make another word. Some can be rearranged more than once. Write the new word or words next to each one.

mug ....

pan ....

pot ....

bowl ....

sink ....

trays ....

stove ....

plate ....

table ....

Alphabet code

Each number represents a letter of the alphabet.
Can you break the code to complete the sentence?
Some letters have been filled in for you.

12	4	4	19
M			

12	4

8	13
	N

19	7	4

15	26	17	10
	A		K

The right word

Which of the two words in bold will fill the blank in each of the sentences? Only one of the words will make sense.

1. I need to check the .... forecast.
weather/whether

2. No boys are .... in our club.
aloud/allowed

3. The dog circled around, chasing its ....
tale/tail

4. The Romans built a .... on the hill.
fort/fought

5. The lion caught its .... within seconds.
prey/pray

6. She handed me a carrot to ....
grate/great

7. The captain called for the .... to be raised.
sale/sail

Word cross

Use the clues at the bottom of the page to find four words that end with the letter 'D'. Then, write their letters in the blank boxes.

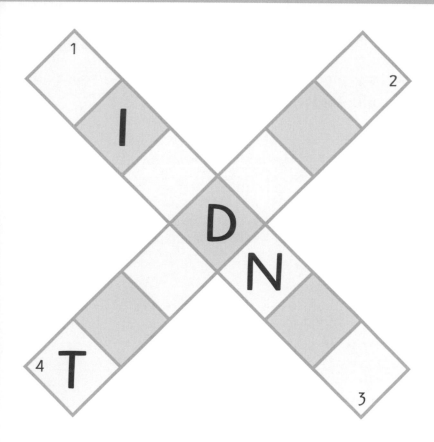

Clues

1. Another word for untamed

2. Having no hair

3. To fix

4. An amphibian

Weather match

Draw lines pairing up the syllables to make words to do with the weather.

blizz	shine
sun	ers
show	ard
cli	zzle
dri	clone
rain	mate
cy	fall

Word triangle

In each section of the triangle, write a word that can be
made by adding one letter to the word above. Use the
clues to help you.

Clues

1. You can use this to cook food in.

2. Scheme, think about how to do something

3. A flying machine

4. An object in space that travels around the Sun

Silhouette fill-in

Look at the silhouettes below, then write the names of the animals into the grid.

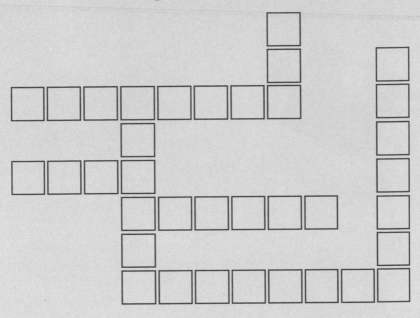

Pair up

All but one of these words can be paired up with another one that has the **same** meaning. Circle the word that is on its own.

boat

mutineer

sailor

vessel

chase

rebel

casket

bounty

pursuit

chest

reward

Solve and search

Solve the clues below, then find the answers hidden in the rings of letters.

1. Large
2. Opposite of east
3. To divide into two equal pieces
4. A creepy-crawly with eight legs
5. Sweet food traditionally eaten on birthdays
6. Winged creature in stories that carries a magic wand

Word sets

Each word set is made up of three words that are related to each other. For example, the words 'high', 'higher' and 'highest' would make up one set, and 'big', 'bigger' and 'biggest' would make up another. Circle the words that **aren't** part of a complete set.

further

worse

less

better

good

worst

best

little

bad

far

furthest

Word detector

1. Which of these words means 'courage'?

SETTLE

HECKLE

METTLE

MEDDLE

METAL

FETTLE

2. Which of these words means 'to lengthen something'?

EXTENT

EXTINCT

EXTEND

EXTRACT

EXTREME

EXTRA

3. Which of these words means 'lean back'?

DECLINE SUBLIME

ALIGN

RECLINE

REFINE MALIGN

4. Which of these words means 'dislike'?

CONSTRAIN

OBTAIN DETAIN

ATTAIN DISDAIN

ABSTAIN

Plant anagrams

These words are anagrams – in each one, the letters can be rearranged to make another word. Some can be rearranged more than once. Write the new word or words next to each one.

bud ....

sap ....

cone ....

vine ....

leaf ....

nuts ....

shoot ....

shrub ....

stalk ....

petal ....

Missing middle

The middles of the words on the left have been removed.
Draw a line to join each word to its missing middle on
the right.

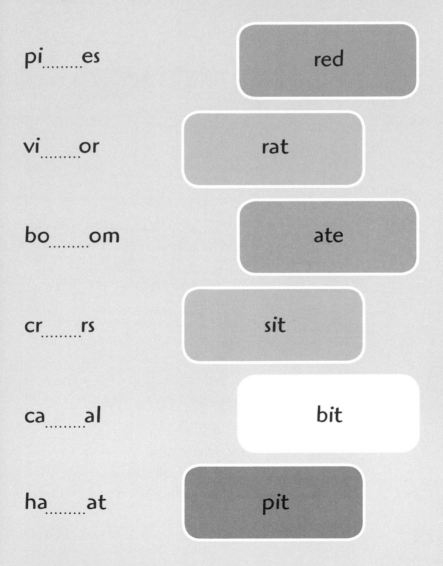

pi........es

vi........or

bo........om

cr........rs

ca........al

ha........at

red

rat

ate

sit

bit

pit

Word stack

Complete the stack by following the clues below. Each word must contain all the letters from the previous word.

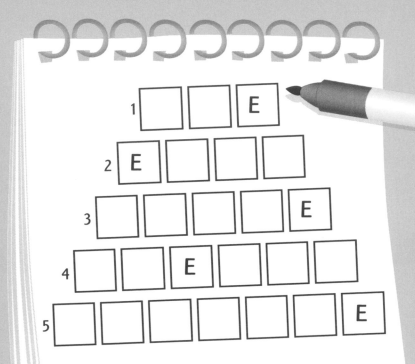

1. E
2. E
3. E
4. E
5. E

Clues

1. A pastry crust with a filling

2. A long, dramatic story or movie

3. This makes food taste 'hot'.

4. "Squawk!.................of eight!"

5. When the sun is cast in shade

Sailing words

Find **eight** words to do with sailing hidden on this boat.

Sound-alikes

Complete each sentence by writing words in the spaces. The words in the two spaces will sound the same, but have different spellings and meanings. The first one has been done for you.

1. You must ......*write*...... the ......*right*...... words in the blank spaces.

2. She had already .... the .... in the trailer for the movie.

3. When she .... the ball, it went straight .... the hoop.

4. After he was .... speeding, he had to go to ....

5. Only .... student .... the top prize.

6. The .... the bed in the hotel room.

Balloon burst

The balloons below will burst if they contain a verb.
Cross out the balloons that will pop.

Middle split

Under each word, write a letter that you can insert to split it into two words, one that ends with the letter and one that starts with it. For example, you can add a T in the middle of BEAN to make BET and TAN. Draw an arrow to show where the letter would go. The first one has been done for you.

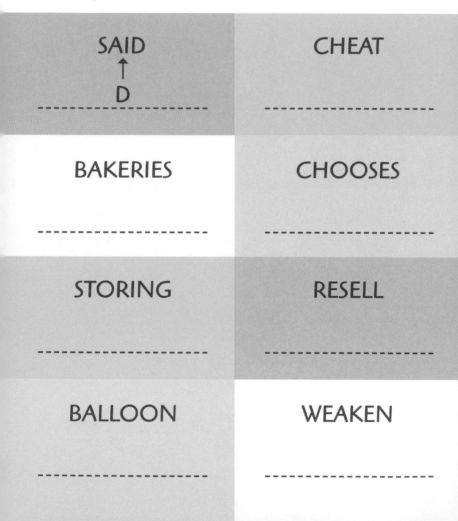

SAID
↑
D
- - - - - - - - - - - - - - - - - - -

CHEAT
- - - - - - - - - - - - - - - - - - -

BAKERIES
- - - - - - - - - - - - - - - - - - -

CHOOSES
- - - - - - - - - - - - - - - - - - -

STORING
- - - - - - - - - - - - - - - - - - -

RESELL
- - - - - - - - - - - - - - - - - - -

BALLOON
- - - - - - - - - - - - - - - - - - -

WEAKEN
- - - - - - - - - - - - - - - - - - -

Food find it

Look at the pictures below, then try to find the names of the food in the grid.

H	M	U	S	H	R	O	O	M	K	A
T	O	R	R	A	Z	Z	I	P	O	C
I	O	S	A	N	D	W	I	C	H	S
T	A	W	K	T	I	O	Z	G	G	T
C	R	T	P	O	C	H	E	E	S	E
P	A	A	G	R	H	S	A	N	L	G
D	R	K	G	R	L	U	W	P	P	L
E	E	S	E	A	P	M	P	I	Z	A
K	R	R	A	C	H	A	K	A	C	M

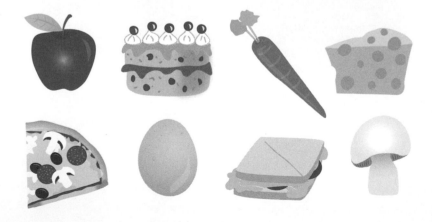

Opposite pairs

All but one of these words can be paired up with another one that has the **opposite** meaning. Circle the word that is on its own.

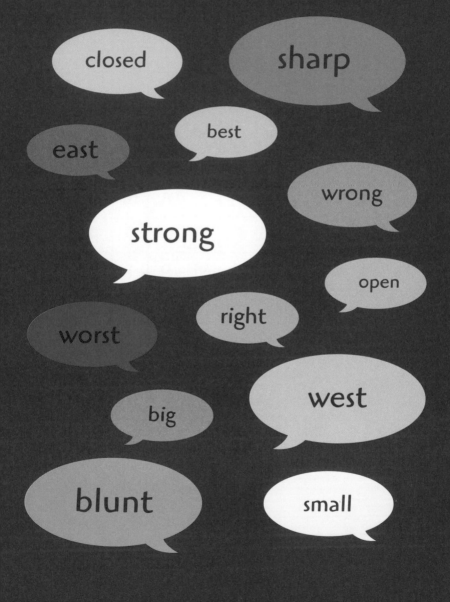

Hexagons

Solve the clues, then write each of the six-letter answers in the grid, following a clockwise path around the clue number. Three letters have been filled in for you.

1. They make bread and cakes.
2. To pretend something isn't there
3. A tune
4. Tired

Vowel Devourer

The Vowel Devourer has stolen all the vowels from these words. Write in the missing letters as quickly as you can before he eats them up.

CR...... T .. R ......

...... M .. Z ......

K ...... P ......

S ......

T .. BL ......

B .. L ...... V ......

D ...... GH

E

A O I U

Eat your words

Each word at the bottom of the page completes one of the phrases on the blackboard. Write the correct phrase number next to each one.

Welcome

1. You are ▓▓▓ you eat.
2. Eat, drink and be ▓▓▓ .
3. Let ▓▓▓ eat cake.
4. Eat to live ▓▓▓ live to eat.
5. I ▓▓▓ eat a horse.
6. Have ▓▓▓ cake and eat it.

.... them   .... could   .... your

.... what   .... merry   .... not

Corner diamonds

Fill the corner diamonds with four of the letters in the middle to make words reading across and down. You may only use each letter once. Circle the letter that's not used.

Sunflower growing

These sentences have become jumbled up. Write the numbers in the order the sentences should appear.

1. Keep watering and weeding the soil every few days.

2. Water the soil where you've just planted the seed.

3. Find a sunny place.

4. Your baby sunflower should appear between one and two weeks after planting.

5. Plant the seed in the soil.

Answer: ....

Word link

Can you fit the words at the bottom into the boxes to complete the chains? As you read down the chains, each pair of words should create a new word.

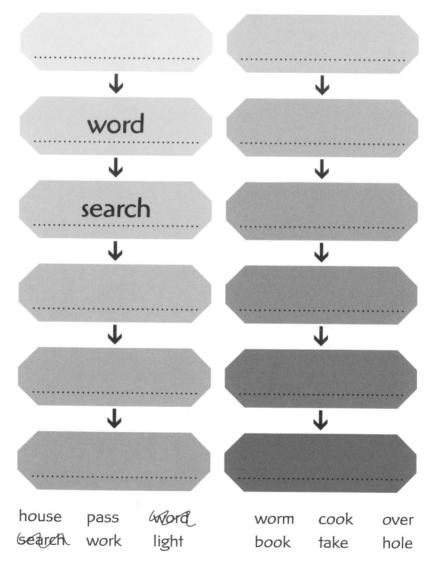

word

search

house   pass   word

search   work   light

worm   cook   over

book   take   hole

Connecting words

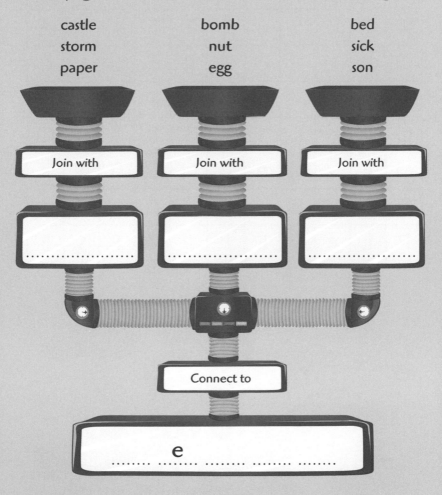

For each list, there is a word that can be added to all three words to create new words. Work out the word for each list, and write it on the blank screen underneath. The words you've written are things that are connected to a type of place. Write the place on the screen at the bottom of the page. One of the letters has been filled in for you.

castle
storm
paper

bomb
nut
egg

bed
sick
son

Join with

Join with

Join with

Connect to

e

Vehicle find it

Look at the pictures below, then try to find the names of
the vehicles in the grid.

U	T	O	N	K	G	C	V	L	F	T
B	U	D	C	I	P	S	U	B	A	R
W	C	U	S	B	L	T	E	I	N	A
O	R	Y	R	O	A	R	I	C	K	C
T	A	T	M	G	N	A	T	Y	I	T
O	P	A	R	S	X	I	R	A	D	O
M	F	V	M	A	B	N	O	P	N	R
G	K	H	B	I	C	Y	C	L	E	K
P	L	A	N	E	L	P	T	F	S	E

Arctic alphabets

There are letters of the alphabet missing from the iceberg. Arrange the missing letters to spell the name of an Arctic animal.

Answer: ....

Stepping stones

Can you change 'head' to 'foot'? Fill the blank stepping stones by changing one letter from the word on the previous stone to form a new word.

1. head

2. bead

3.

4.

5.

6. foot

Find eight words with **four** or more letters hidden in the grid. One word uses all nine letters. You can move from letter to letter by going up, down, left, right or diagonally – but you can't jump over a square. Names, and words ending in 's', don't count, and you can't use the same letter twice in a word.

1. ....

2. ....

3. ....

4. ....

5. ....

6. ....

7. ....

8. ....

Wordplays

The grid is made up of nine blocks, each containing nine squares. Fill in the blank squares, so that each block, row and column contains all the letters of the word WORDPLAYS.

			W	P			A	
W		L				Y	O	
R			Y	L			D	
S			D			P	L	A
		D	A		Y	R		
A	R	O			L			D
	D			Y	W			S
	W	A				O		Y
	P			R	A			

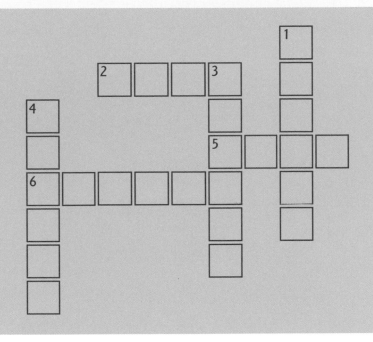

Pets crossword

The answers to the clues are all to do with pets. Solve the clues and write your answers in the grid.

Across

2. You can take a dog for one of these.

5. You can keep a fish in this.

6. You can keep this pet in a hutch.

Down

1. .... pig

3. A baby cat

4. You can teach this pet to say words.

Step words

Write a word on each step by rearranging the letters in the word above, plus adding an extra one. Follow the clues to write the correct words. The first two steps have been completed for you.

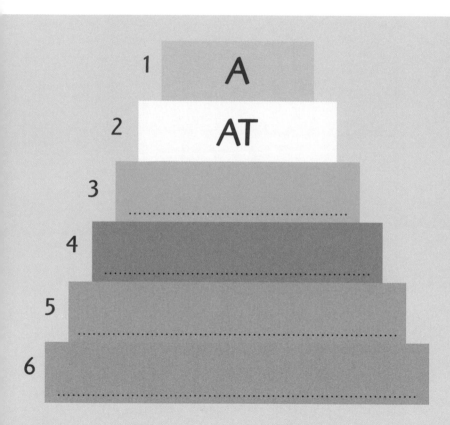

1   A

2   AT

3   ....

4   ....

5   ....

6   ....

Clues

1. First letter of the alphabet

2. @

3. Hot drink

4. Friend

5. Hard substance

6. About the mind

Circle words

Make as many three-letter words as you can from the letters below, using one letter from each circle. The first letter must be from circle 1, the second from circle 2, and the last from circle 3. How many words can be made?

1
R   D
    L

2
A   E
    I

3
W   N
    T

....

....

Answer: ....

Castle search

Can you find the words below hidden in this castle-shaped grid?

M	P		Q	T		N	D		W	T
O	F		U	H		S	I		A	H
I	S	A	L	G	K	W	R	O	F	S
T	W	N	A	I	T	O	M	G	C	H
E	O	L	N	N	Q	U	E	E	N	I
G	F	W	C	K	I	N	L	I	R	E
N	S	E	E	T	M	C	O	E	L	L
I	E	H	S	R	R	S	W	O	R	D
E	I	E	D				Q	U	T	O
U	U	G	P				G	N	I	K
Q	T	N	O				D	H	S	N

MOAT   KING   QUEST

KNIGHT   LANCE   SHIELD

SWORD   TOWER   QUEEN

Letter tiles

Write the letters on the tiles in the grid to make words reading across and down. Follow the layout of the letters on the tiles, so that if two letters are one under the other on a tile, you must write them one under the other in the grid. Two tiles have been copied into the grid for you.

Animal words

The words on the left each describe an animal. For example, 'feline' means cat-like. Draw a line between each word and its picture.

leonine

bovine

feline

equine

canine

vulpine

serpentine

Corner circles

Fill the corner circles with four of the letters in the middle
to make words across and down. You can only use each
letter once. Circle the letter that's not used.

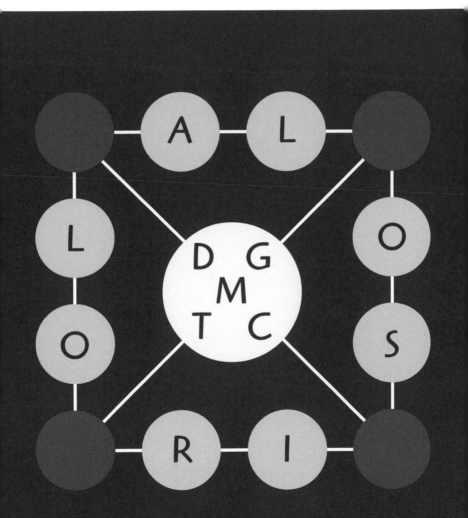

Pearl fishing

The oyster shells will snap shut if you try to harvest the pearls that have adjectives written on them. Circle the pearls that are safe to take.

shiny

storm

take

danger

shell

small

Word flower

Solve the clues and write the words on the petals.
Each word ends with the letter 'L', and one word
has been completed for you.

Clues

1. Found in alarms

2. Chilly

3. Opposite of good

4. Orange skin

5. Two-person fight

6. Opposite of succeed

7. Make better

8. Furry sea mammal

Sweet rhymes

Circle the word that doesn't rhyme with any of the others.

eat

bite

scoffed

two

sweet

tough

chew

through

treat

soft

delight

Compass points

Use the compass directions below to find the correct locations for the missing letters. When you have filled in all the letters, see if you can discover the hidden names of three well-known rivers.

```
A   D   S   I   D   Y
C   M   S   E   L   T
... Y   ... O   ... A   I   C
I   T   M   ... N   N   R   Y
... A   R   S   O   I   A   K
E   V   M   A   B   ...   P   ...
```

Write a **G** in a space that is South of an L.
Write an **L** in a space that is North of an E.
Write a **Z** in a space that is East of an M.
Write an **N** in a space that is West of a P.
Write an **A** in a space that is East of a Y.
Write a **G** in a space that is South of a K.
Write an **N** in a space that is North of an I.

Spy code

Secret Agent X has received a coded message from his boss. To break the code, you have to:

- Remove the spaces between the letters.
- Reverse the order of the letters, so that you can read them from left to right.
- Divide the letters into words.

What do the coded sentences say? The first one has been done for you.

1. slla cruo yotn etsi lnac yehT

   They can listen to your calls

2. enoh pruo yyor tseD

   ....

   ....

3. snoi tcur tsni reht ruft iawA

   ....

   ....

Hidden animals

Underline the name of a wild animal hidden in each sentence. The first one has been done for you.

1. She's tal**l: I, on** the other hand, am short.

2. He found the lost riches of Eldorado.

3. Where on Earth are you?

4. This naked flame could burn you.

5. He became a movie buff a long time ago.

6. She was on the ship, posing for the cameras.

7. He arrived with yen and dollars in his wallet.

8. The paths of the maze branched out in all directions.

Precious stone search

Can you find the words below hidden in this grid?

PEARL

RUBY

GEM

OPAL

JADE

TOPAZ

CORAL

AMBER

A
A M
Y E B
S G R E
K J B U R
O P A L B L
R A L D A Y X
C O R E L T
O Z A M Z
R L E A
A N P
L O
T

Odd word out

Underline the word in each list that is the odd one out.

1. spotted
   dotted
   banded
   patchy
   splotchy

2. cold
   tepid
   bitter
   chilly
   frosty

3. glittering
   sparkling
   shiny
   dusky
   gleaming

4. running
   racing
   dashing
   sprinting
   ambling

5. bounding
   gliding
   bouncing
   jumping
   leaping

6. happy
   cheerful
   morose
   glad
   content

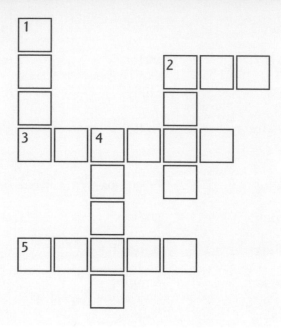

Summer crossword

The answers to the clues are all to do with summer.
Solve the clues and write your answers in the grid.

Across

2. This shines in the sky.

3. A meal eaten outside

5. A sandy place beside the sea

Down

1. You sleep in a tent when you do this.

2. Move through water

4. A cold dessert, ice...........

Sports match

Draw lines pairing up the syllables to make sports words.

foot   is

hock   board

tenn   ball

score   tain

cap   er

play   cling

cy   ey

Sea jumble

The words in each line can be rearranged to make a sentence. Write numbers under the words to show their correct order, writing '1' under the first, and so on.

1. storm. sank a in ship violent The

....

2. was of king's the All lost. treasure

....

3. the An cabin. angry in lives monster

....

Fishy puzzle

In each row of words, there is one letter that appears only once. Collect these letters and shuffle them to spell out the name of a type of underwater creature.

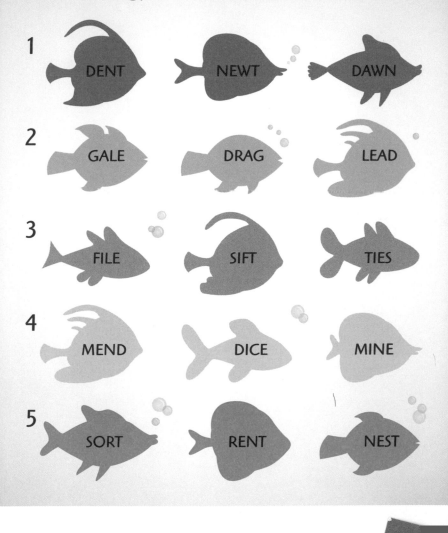

1   DENT   NEWT   DAWN

2   GALE   DRAG   LEAD

3   FILE   SIFT   TIES

4   MEND   DICE   MINE

5   SORT   RENT   NEST

Answer: ....

Alien words

Draw a circle around the words that **can't** be made from the letters in the word ALIENS using each letter only once.

SAIL

LINE   SNAIL

LOANS

AISLE   STALE

SEAL

RAIN

LEANS

SANE

LIKE

LIE

Out of order

Write numbers next to these words to put them in alphabetical order. The first and last ones have been done for you.

reorder

revolve

remain

9 reward

review

rehearse

remember

regain 1

regards

Orange alert

How many times does the word ORANGE appear in these letters?

```
            O R O R A
          G E R R N O R A
        E G N A R O A R O E
      O N E N E O N O R G R A
    A R O G O O G R A N O O R A
    N A E N R E G N A R O R O N
  E E N O A A O G R A N O A E G O
  R G G N R N E O N O R A N G E N
  O N E O O G R O O A N O G N O A
  R A R O N E R E O R R A E A R G
  A R O O R A N A G R A O R R A E
    O E G N A R O O N G N O O N
    A A G R O N O O R A N G E G
      E O R A N G E R O R G N E
      R A N G E O E O A N O E
        N O R A N G E G O
          O N R E A
```

Answer: ....

Mirror words

Draw the mirror image of these symbols to complete the words. The first one has been done for you.

WOW   TU

OT   id

CHECK   DECIDE

COOKBOOK

Word link

Can you fit the words at the bottom into the boxes to complete the chains? As you read down the chains, each pair of words should create a new word.

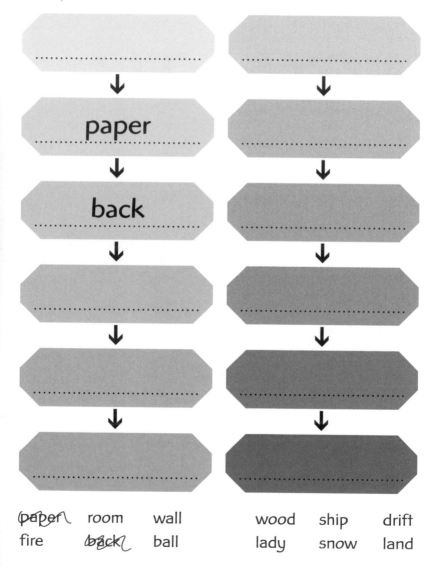

paper

back

paper   room   wall

fire   back   ball

wood   ship   drift

lady   snow   land

Safari scramble

Can you unscramble these groups of letters to find the names of six animals you might see on safari?

1. fairfeg	4. theache ....
2. thenplea	5. polared ....
3. lograil	6. clorecoid ....

Musical fill-in

Write the names of the musical instruments below into the grid.

Words in a word

Use the clues below to find some of the words that can be made from the letters in TRANSFORMATIONS. No letter can be used more than the number of times it appears in the original word.

1. ....
Clue: A simple, flat boat (4 letters)

2. ....
Clue: A thin layer of ice; Jack .... (5 letters)

3. ....
Clue: A red fruit used in salads (6 letters)

4. ....
Clue: A large house (7 letters)

5. ....
Clue: Places where trains stop (8 letters)

First and last

Each of these words starts and ends with the same letter.
Can you fill in the missing letters?

.... ATC ....

...........ARGE...........

.... EGA ....

.... USEU...........

.... ROM...........

...........ALLO...........

.... AGL ....

.... LINI ....

.... UTD ....

.... ATIO...........

Building sandcastles

These sentences have become jumbled up. Write the numbers in the order the sentences should appear.

1. Build an impressive sandcastle with lots of towers.

2. Make a pile of sand, and flatten it down for a base.

3. Dig a moat all around your completed sandcastle.

4. Fill a bucket with wet sand and turn it over to make a tower.

5. Decorate all the towers with shells and pebbles.

Answer: ....

Fragments

The grid is made up of nine blocks, each containing nine squares. Fill in the blank squares, so that each block, row and column contains all the letters of the word FRAGMENTS.

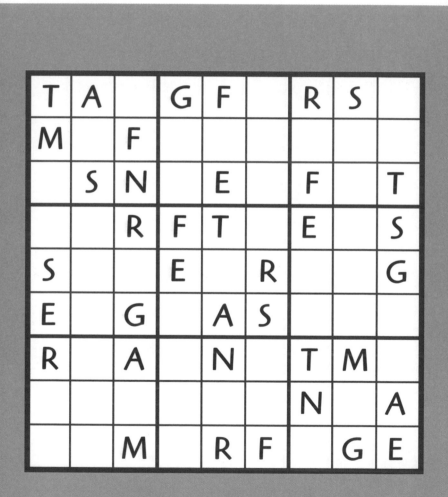

Hidden fruits

Underline the name of a fruit hidden in each sentence.
The first one has been done for you.

1. Take off your **cap, ple**ase.

2. Mr. Orlando ran geology club today.

3. Never grab an anaconda by its tail!

4. There's no such thing as a gentle monster.

5. I howled, but the wolf ignored me.

6. The pope achieved a lot in his lifetime.

7. I always find this café's soup lumpy.

8. The old woman got very confused.

Rainforest jumble

There are letters of the alphabet missing from this rainforest scene. Arrange the missing letters to find out which animal is hiding amongst the trees.

Answer: ....

Answers

1. Word ladder:

starting, staring, string, sting, sing

2. Pirate challenge:

plate, ten, rare, pest, area

3. Word wheel:

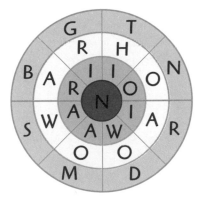

4. Shape fill-in:

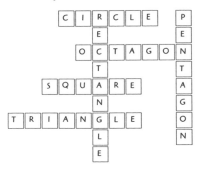

5. Blog entry:

Today my dad was angry becouse I spendt my lunch money on a tenis ball. Nowon has a tenis ball. They always get losed so everyone will play with my ball. We had stu for diner. Yuck. Then I went to Neil's house and plade computer games. He always beets me but today I beet him. He said he losed on purpus. More scool tomoro.

6. Written in the stars:

constellations

7. Word swirl: 24

Answers

8. Word web:

try, fly, sky

9. Broken words: ter

10. Duplicate:

D	L	U	I	T	P	E	C	A
E	A	I	C	L	D	U	P	T
T	P	C	E	U	A	I	D	L
U	D	L	P	A	I	C	T	E
P	E	A	T	C	U	D	L	I
I	C	T	D	E	L	P	A	U
L	U	P	A	I	C	T	E	D
A	T	D	U	P	E	L	I	C
C	I	E	L	D	T	A	U	P

11. Camping crossword:

12. Opposites attract:

bossy

13. Spelling spotter:

My heroe is Robbin Hood. He took monney from rich people who woudn't share even thow poor people were really hungry. He robed the rich to fede the por and campt out every nite with his frends in a big forest caled Sherwood. I wish he was alive 2day so we cud lite a fir and sing songs and I woud tell evryone that I was frends with Robbin Hood.

14. Ice hopping:

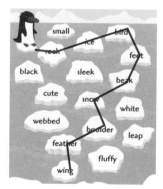

15. Word switch:

1. gear, gate

2. hole, hint

3. mule, more

4. pass, page

5. sold, soil

6. tray, trap

16. Puzzle planet:

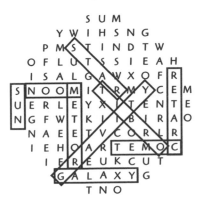

17. Words in a word:
1. song   2. trail   3. signal
4. against   5. cartoons

18. Daisy chain:
seed, send, lend,
lead, leaf

19. Double meanings:
1. live   2. records   3. bow
4. rose

20. First and last:

comic	mayhem
loyal	defend
erase	widow
trust	kiosk
arena	fluff

21. Cross e-word:

22. Word pairs: light

23. Butterfly maze:
flutter

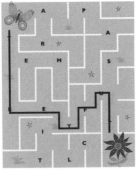

24. Odd one out:
1. loitering   2. alert
3. ignore   4. bright
5. racket   6. rush

25. Which word?:
1. hazard   2. strive
3. fuchsia   4. fraction

Answers

26. Space scramble:

1. planet 2. rocket
3. astronaut 4. asteroid
5. satellite 6. meteorite

27. Corner letters:

You can make any of
these words: daylight,
daylit, tidal, daily,
laid, dial, lady,
glad

28. Farm jumble:

1 - 5, 4, 2, 1, 3
2 - 2, 4, 6, 5, 1, 3
3 - 6, 2, 5, 3, 1, 7, 4

29. Front and back:

maintain, relevant,
highland, sizzling,
nominate

30. Book words:

1. hand 2. work
3. worm 4. case

31. Hidden insects:

1. I found the m**ap hid**den
below deck.
2. I won't be coming;
I'**m oth**erwise engaged.
3. The tri**be e**xpected their
new leader to be strong.
4. The boy **was p**laying his
guitar upstairs.
5. He r**an to** the other side.
6. She has a stall
sellin**g nat**ural
and organic cosmetics.
7. The b**ear wig**gled as
it danced.
8. He had to sti**fle a** yawn
as he pretended to listen.

32. Coded message:

Answers

33. Lily pads:

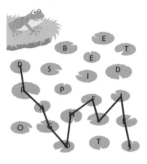

34. Cat rescue:

cat, tree, house, plan, face, help, head, held, high

35. Beach scramble:

1. sandcastle 2. seashell
3. starfish 4. jellyfish
5. rockpool 6. seaweed

36. Kitchen anagrams:

gum, nap, top/opt, blow, skin/inks, stray, votes, pleat/petal/leapt, bleat

37. Alphabet code:

Meet me in the park

38. The right word:

1. weather 2. allowed
3. tail 4. fort 5. prey
6. grate 7. sail

39. Word cross:

1. wild 2. bald
3. mend 4. toad

40. Weather match:

blizzard, sunshine, showers, climate, drizzle, rainfall, cyclone

41. Word triangle:

1. pan 2. plan 3.plane
4. planet

42. Silhouette fill-in:

43. Pair up: sailor

44. Solve and search:

45. Word sets:
less, little

46. Word detector:
1. mettle 2. extend
3. recline 4. disdain

47. Plant anagrams:
dub, asp/spa, once, vein,
flea, stun, hoots/sooth,
brush, talks, plate/pleat/leapt

48. Missing middle:
pirates, visitor, boredom,
craters, capital, habitat

49. Word stack:
1. pie 2. epic 3. spice
4. pieces 5. eclipse

50. Sailing words:

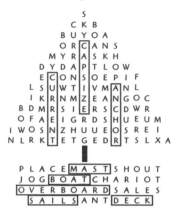

51. Sound-alikes:
1. write/right
2. seen/scene
3. threw/through
4. caught/court
5. one/won
6. maid/made

52. Balloon burst:
celebrate, Be mine,
I love you

53. Middle split:
sad did, chef fat,
baked dries, chop poses,
stork king, rest tell,
balls soon, wet taken

54. Food find it:

55. Opposite pairs: strong

56. Hexagons:

57. Vowel Devourer:
creature, amaze, keep, suitable, believe, dough

58. Eat your words:
3 them, 5 could, 6 your, 1 what, 2 merry, 4 not

59. Corner diamonds:

60. Sunflower growing:
3, 5, 2, 1, 4

61. Word link:

pass	take
word	over
search	cook
light	book
house	worm
work	hole

62. Connecting words:

63. Vehicle find it:

64. Arctic alphabets:
walrus

65. Stepping stones:
head, bead, beat, boat, boot, foot

Answers

66. Word trail:

You can make any of these:
arise, arisen, base, basin, main, marine, rain, raise, rinse, rise, risen, sari, snub, submarine

67. Wordplays:

D	O	Y	W	P	S	L	A	R
W	S	L	R	A	D	Y	O	P
R	A	P	Y	L	O	S	D	W
S	Y	W	D	O	R	P	L	A
P	L	D	A	W	Y	R	S	O
A	R	O	P	S	L	W	Y	D
O	D	R	L	Y	W	A	P	S
L	W	A	S	D	P	O	R	Y
Y	P	S	O	R	A	D	W	L

68. Pets crossword:

69. Step words:

1. a   2. at   3. tea   4. mate
5. metal   6. mental

70. Circle words:

9

(den, dew, din, law, let, lit, ran, rat, raw)

71. Castle search:

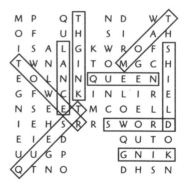

72. Letter tiles:

73. Animal words:

leonine/lion, bovine/cow, feline/cat, equine/horse, canine/dog, vulpine/fox, serpentine/snake

74. Corner circles:

C A L M

L D O

O S

G R I T

75. Pearl fishing:

storm, take, shell, danger

76. Word flower:

77. Sweet rhymes:

tough

78. Compass points:

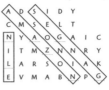

79. Spy code:

1. They can listen to your calls
2. Destroy your phone
3. Await further instructions

80. Hidden animals:

1. She's tal**l: I, on** the other hand, am short.
2. He found the l**ost rich**es of Eldorado.
3. Where on Eart**h are** you?
4. Thi**s nake**d flame could burn you.
5. He became a movie **buff a lo**ng time ago.
6. She was on the s**hip, po**sing for the cameras.
7. He arrived wit**h yen a**nd dollars in his wallet.
8. The paths of the ma**ze bra**nched out in all directions.

81. Precious stone search:

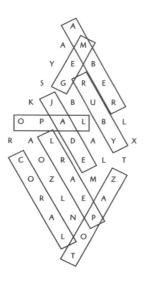

82. Odd word out:

1. banded   2. tepid
3. dusky   4. ambling
5. gliding   6. morose

83. Summer crossword:

84. Sports match:

foot — tain
hock — ball
tenn — is
score — board
cap — ey
play — er
cy — cling

85. Sea jumble:

1 - 7, 3, 5, 4, 2, 6, 1
2 - 6, 2, 4, 3, 1, 7, 5
3 - 6, 1, 7, 2, 5, 4, 3

86. Fishy puzzle:

coral

87. Alien words:

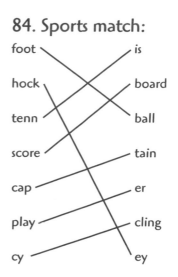

Answers

88. Out of order:

1. regain 2. regards
3. rehearse 4. remain
5. remember 6. reorder
7. review 8. revolve
9. reward

89. Orange alert: 22

90. Mirror words:

TUT

TOOT **bid**

CHECK **DECIDE**

COOKBOOK

91. Word link:

wall snow
paper drift
back wood
fire land
ball lady
room ship

92. Safari scramble:

1. giraffe 2. elephant
3. gorilla 4. cheetah
5. leopard 6. crocodile

93. Musical fill-in:

94. Words in a word:

1. raft 2. frost 3. tomato
4. mansion 5. stations

Answers

95. First and last:

hatch	target
legal	museum
aroma	wallow
eagle	clinic
outdo	nation

96. Building sandcastles:

2, 4, 1, 5, 3

97. Fragments:

T	A	E	G	F	N	R	S	M
M	R	F	T	S	A	G	E	N
G	S	N	R	E	M	F	A	T
A	M	R	F	T	G	E	N	S
S	N	T	E	M	R	A	F	G
E	F	G	N	A	S	M	T	R
R	G	A	S	N	E	T	M	F
F	E	S	M	G	T	N	R	A
N	T	M	A	R	F	S	G	E

98. Hidden fruits:

1. Take off your c**ap, ple**ase.
2. Mr. Orland**o ran ge**ology club today.
3. Never gra**b an ana**conda by its tail!
4. There's no such thing as a gent**le mon**ster.
5. I howled, but the wol**f ig**nored me.
6. The po**pe ach**ieved a lot in his lifetime.
7. I always find this café's sou**p lum**py.
8. The old wo**man go**t very confused.

99. Rainforest jumble:

panther